THE SEDUCTION GAME

Courtesy of Intanon Pictures

Charlie Nawamin

THE SEDUCTION GAME

Author: Charlie Nawamin

ISBN : 978-616-612-224-4
ISBN(e-book) : 978-616-612-145-2

First edition March 2024
Published by Chalart Sriwanna

Front cover: Courtesy of Intanon Pictures

Dedicated to all the remarkable cast and crew members,

Your dedication, talent, and passion brought the magic of "The Seduction Game" to life on the screen, captivating audiences with every frame. Now, as this beloved story makes its transition from film to book, your contributions continue to inspire and shape its journey. This book is a testament to the incredible teamwork and creativity that made the film possible. Thank you for your unwavering commitment and for sharing your brilliance with the world.

With deepest appreciation,
Charlie Nawamin

My Other Books

Untold Bedtime Stories: From the Far East
The Loyal Trio: Wings of Trust and Friendship
Kaya's Triump: A Tale of Courage and Unity
The Watcher Ghost
The Tale of Two Souls
Golden Fields of Love
The Waters of Change*
The Swineherd who Rescued the Princess*
Whispers of Resilience*
The IQ Box*
The Rebirth of Niran*
The Lost Kingdom of Love*
The Unwavering Threads of Destiny*
Karmic Reflections of Love

*Certain volumes of my books aren't available for purchase; rather, they are crafted with the sole purpose of being donated as educational treasures for less fortunate children. Most of them have been curated into a collective anthology under the enchanting title, "Untold Bedtime Stories from the Far East."

CHAPTER ONE

The gentle tapping of the keyboard resonates through a house nestled in a distant, serene forest. Twatchai, a young man on the cusp of 30, is immersed in the creation of the final chapters of his latest novel. The interior of his new, spacious dwelling hints at his recent relocation. The rhythmic keystrokes harmonize seamlessly with the ambient jazz music, creating a unique atmosphere within the house. Before long, pages filled with text gracefully emerge from the printer, each one bearing the culmination of his literary endeavors.

Stepping outside, he carries himself with an effortless grace, whistling in tune with the melody that has just concluded. With a heart full of satisfaction, he ascends into his pickup truck, driving away from the house with a buoyant spirit. The narrow, meandering road descent from the hill poses a challenge to cellphone signals. He raises his phone, observing the sparse signal, a lone and delicate bar. Aware of potential communication difficulties, he decides to place the call.

'Hello Onn, I'm on my way... Hello... hello…' The signal disappears just as the conversation is getting started. Eventually, as he approaches a small, quaint gas station, the signal strengthens. He dials Onn's number again.

'My apologies. Signal troubles. Yes, I'm on my way. Should arrive by noon.' After a journey of just over two hours on the road, Twatchai's car gracefully enters the vibrant city of Bangkok. The urban ambiance buzzes with the orchestrated chaos of the congested traffic. He strolls into the printing house, where the resounding echoes of printing presses fill the air. Tranquility envelops him as he enters the glass-walled office of Onn, the publishing manager—a poised woman in her forties, her long, elegantly arranged dark hair adding to her allure. They exchange warm pleasantries.

'You're running a bit behind for lunch. Otherwise, I would've treated you to a meal.' Onn breaks the silence that follows the initial exchange of greetings.

'Aw, that's sweet of you. How about switching it to dinner?' proposed Twatchai.

'Not possible. Evenings are reserved for my boy's loving daddy.'

'Ah, seems a hint of envy for someone with a family.'

'Speak as if you're still single. Don't you have a family yourself?' Twatchai chuckles with a twinkle in his eye, inviting Onn to join in the laughter. Onn hands over the check she has prepared for him. Once he receives the check, he swiftly proposes a new creative piece, eager to divert the conversation.

'Yet, I have another story I'd like to propose.'

'Oh, what kind of genre?'

'Crime story, as always.' Onn, uninterested in delving into the plot details, remains silent for a moment before outright rejecting it.

'This genre isn't working anymore. Sales have consistently been poor. It's just not gaining traction. What I'm saying is this will be the last one we publish.' Onn's clear and direct response briefly catches Twatchai off guard before he manages to share his thoughts.

'But I'm not skilled in any other genre.'

'Have a go at integrating some sexuality into it.'

'Erotic?' Twatchai's voice wavers, betraying a hint of uncertainty that lingers in the air. With confidence, Onn responds.

'The market is moving in that direction. Why not give it a try?'

'Well, it's a challenge. Alter the writing approach a bit to avoid repetition.'

'Any working title yet? I can schedule it for you now.'

'I'll let you know once I come up with it.'

Twatchai is an emerging writer with a unique flair for storytelling. Recognizing his strengths, he acknowledges the importance of Onn's mentorship, particularly in navigating the complexities of the market. Despite their recent acquaintance and collaboration on only a few occasions, working together on four books penned by Twatchai for Onn's publishing house, the two foster a warm and friendly relationship that gives the impression of a longstanding connection.

'Have I told you I sold my house, the one in Bangkok?' It's time for Twatchai to break the silence.

'Congratulations! So, your wife finally gave

her approval for the sale, right?'

'Yeah, we came to an agreement. After finishing up here, I'll drop by her mom and pick her up.'

'She'll love it. Believe me. I, myself, aspire to relocate to such a tranquil place. The air there is incredibly refreshing.'

It's a sentiment experienced by nearly everyone in the city who yearns to escape the bustling pace of Bangkok, often dedicating long weekends to travel and find solace in the mountains or at some secluded beach. Twatchai's profession as a writer grants him the luxury of not being tethered to a bustling city. He considers himself fortunate compared to many others. While his young spouse has acclimated to the comforts of city life, she harbors concerns about uprooting to a new and unfamiliar locale.

'If you ever consider selling it, please inform me first.' Onn's words carry a blend of playful banter and genuine sincerity, echoing a nuanced sentiment in the air.

'If I sell this one, I don't know where I'll go.'

The couple exchanges playful banter for a while before the ringing of the telephone on the desk interrupts them. Twatchai senses that it is time to bid farewell to Onn, considering that he has taken up enough of her time.

'I should go, and thank you.' He expresses his gratitude while holding up the check.

'I'll be waiting for the new title.' She shouts after Twatchai as he leaves.

CHAPTER TWO

The early morning sunlight filters through the leaves, casting a gentle glow as Nuch rides her bike along the meandering trail. Dressed in well-fitted shorts and a single-strap tank top, her fair complexion with a hint of pink contrasts beautifully with the lush greenery. Nuch enjoys the serene atmosphere of the forest, navigating the twists and turns on her bicycle. Meanwhile, Twatchai sits before his computer, his mind seemingly adrift, much like a cursor on the idle screen. He remains in this contemplative state until Nuch returns home. The newlywed house's interior features an open layout devoid of partitions, a space awaiting the imprint of his creative choices, allowing him to catch the sound of his wife's footsteps upon her return. His thoughts begin to intertwine with reality, envisioning Nuch removing her cap and casually tossing it onto the table. The image of her running her fingers through her hair to alleviate the heat captivates his mind. Every action by Nuch serves as a cue for Twatchai's vivid imagination. He visualizes the gentle sound of his loving wife pouring a refreshing drink into a glass from the fridge, the droplets resonating as they land on her chest, glistening with sweat. He makes an effort to infuse a touch of romance into this mental scenario. As she quenches her thirst with the cool beverage, she carefully places the glass on the counter, and the subsequent absence of movement from her leaves a tranquil ambiance. Nevertheless, the narrative within Twatchai's thoughts continues to unfold.

Nuch appears to be making her way towards the bathroom, according to his imaginative interpretation. The subsequent scenario unfolds with her removing her wet attire and gracefully stepping into the shower, where she stands beneath the flowing water. Twatchai descends slowly from the upper deck, enticed by the faint sound of a shower. The bathroom is the sole space, with a partition next to the kitchen area. As he passes the sink, the glint of a knife catches his attention. Retrieving it, he holds the one-foot-long blade, its sharpness reflecting on his determined expression. The bathroom door is slightly ajar, and without hesitation, he enters. Nuch stands behind the semi-transparent shower curtain, oblivious to the impending danger, as he approaches with the raised knife. His focus remains on the silhouette of her, undressed and unsuspecting, completely unaware of the looming threat.

'Wat... Wat...' The voice of Nuch lingers

in the air. The abbreviated name Twatchai wakes him from his reverie. He notices his wife standing right in front of him, holding a glass of water, following the tradition she has learned since childhood about caring for loved ones. She places the cool water glass on the table before him.

'Are you asleep?'

'Nah, I'm just struggling with my writing.' He quickly dismisses all his imaginative thoughts, seemingly worried that she might sense what he is contemplating.

'Take a break; creativity hits a snag sometimes.'

The subtle fragrance of her perspiration, lingering just within his proximity, instantly catches his desire. He pulls her closer and gazes at her with longing, and she immediately senses his desires.

'Hold on, I need a shower.' But before she can escape, he grabs her wrist, pulling her back. Nothing is restraining his heart at this moment except letting him express his desires. The wife responds by sitting on his lap, and they kiss passionately. He takes off his shorts, and both embrace each other in love. Before long, he reaches the climax and settles in bliss. As the poor wife is about to initiate a tender moment, feeling let down, she chooses to internalize her disappointment and quietly rises, walking away. Twatchai diverts his attention to the empty monitor.

Someone accustomed to the vibrant life of a bustling city might avoid smaller shopping malls in rural areas. Twatchai, however, finds himself inevitably drawn to these stores to buy their daily necessities. Nuch, on the contrary, casually mentions her inclination to stay home and engage in housecleaning.

'You sure you ain't comin' with me?'

'I reckon stayin' home and doin' some cleaning.'

'Worried you might get bored. It's no biggie.'

'I'm tryin' to adapt; no need to fret.' She smiles, letting him know she appreciates his concern. He gives his lovely wife a sweet kiss before heading out.

CHAPTER THREE

The small gas station serves as the starting point where the phone signal begins to reappear. Twatchai often diverts his gaze from the road to check his phone for missed calls or messages. On this remote and deserted stretch of road, he never expects anyone to suddenly appear. The loud impact of the collision causes a body to float over the back of the car and tumble onto the road. Startled, he promptly hits the brakes and peers through the rearview mirror. Initially assuming it might be an animal collision, he doesn't foresee encountering a person. Regaining his composure, he exits the car and hurries to inspect the unmoving figure, uncertain if it's injured or deceased. The surroundings offer no sign of pedestrians or passing vehicles, only the resounding chirps of crickets in the air.

He steers the car back into the driveway, sparking curiosity in his wife about his unexpectedly swift return. Noticing the unusual expression on his face, she senses that something is wrong and quickly approaches. He opens the rear door, exposing a stranger lying inside. Twatchai's frightened demeanor causes concern for Nuch.

'I... I hit him.' His voice quivers with a sense of unease. He sadly faces his wife, but his good intentions only disappoint her. 'Should you take him to the hospital?'

'Nuch, what If he dies, I'll surely be imprisoned.' His voice continues to tremble.

'So you're letting him die in our home?'

The husband, overwhelmed and uncertain about what to do, instinctively reaches out to console her, though he isn't fully aware of the reasons behind his actions. Amidst the chaos, he contemplates something, and he places his hand over the enigmatic man's nose to feel for any signs of breathing.

'He's still breathing.' Twatchai's relief eases her tension a bit, but her anger prompts her to bring up issues with him.

'You're such a troublemaker, always stirring things up.'

'Nuch, this idiot just appeared out of nowhere. I swear to God, I couldn't hit the brakes in time.' A moment of silence lingers between them within the safety of a pause. She breaks the silence and asks a question.

'What's next?'

'Bring him inside for now. I'll have the damn car fixed.'

'No way! I'll not allow you to do that.'

'Now, what am I supposed to do?'

'Dump him in the woods, wherever. I don't know.' They both have no idea that every word they speak reaches the consciousness of the strange man, even though he appears to be unconscious.

'Nuch, if the cops find the body and my car banged up like this, I'll be in deep shit. Gotta ditch the evidence fast, then figure out what to do with the body, alright?' He is making an effort to persuade his wife to go along with his plan. Despite appearing excessively panicked, he has valid reasons that eventually convince her to agree.

'Please do as I say.' Together, the husband and wife bring the stranger into the living room and place him on the sofa. She examines the injuries roughly, drawing on her nursing knowledge to gain a basic understanding that the enigmatic man's condition is not too critical.

'Found a little bump on the head. Doesn't seem like a big deal.'

'Beats me, his body floats across the back of the car.' He vividly remembers the impact when the collision occurs, unsure of how to forget it. He is in a state of turmoil, anxious about the dented front of the car, fearing it might serve as self-incriminating evidence. He is restless, contemplating, and hurriedly considering taking the car for repairs.

'Are you going to leave me alone here with him?'

'I'll get back in a flash, alright?' Nuch, despite her own experiences with the sick and the dying, seems more composed than her husband, who is in a state of panic. So he leaves.

After departing from the residence, Twatchai finds himself uncertain about which auto shop to entrust with the repairs. He is cautious of meddling mechanics and seeks to keep the incident hidden from potential police scrutiny. Being a newcomer to the area, he lacks the companionship of friends or acquaintances who could recommend a reliable shop. Thus, he meanders through the streets, contemplating his options, until the phone rings, with the caller inquiring about the title of the recently discussed book.

'Hey, I'm waiting for the title. Anything temporary?' The genuine voice of Onn resonates over the phone.

'My apologies. I'm in the midst of an accident, trying to find a garage.'

'Looking for an auto body shop? I know a place; best of all, take my recommendation.' It feels like a weight off Twatchai's shoulders.

'Just give me the contact info.'

Onn, serving as both a benefactor and a trusted friend, emerges as Twatchai's guiding light of hope. Onn's thoughtful recommendations illuminate a clear path for him. It merely requires his willingness to undertake the long drive into Bangkok. With this simple act, the intricate threads of the accident's aftermath can begin to unravel.

He parks his car on the roadside, facing the sign indicating "Bangkok 152 kilometers." He gazes ahead contemplatively, carefully weighing his decision before proceeding on the straight path. While Nuch waits for her husband's return, the landline phone rings.

'Hello,' Nuch answers.

'How's everything?'

'Where the hell are you? What took you so long?'

'Listen up. Cops are all over the place. I've decided to head to Bangkok.'

'What?...' She exclaims.

'It's better to handle it far away.'

'Where are you at? Come back right now.' Nuch speaks with a commanding voice, completely negating his terms.

'Sorry, Nuch. I'll hurry back.' her beloved husband promptly ends the call, aware that lingering any longer might hinder his departure.

'God damn you.' Nuch swears. Just as she is about to make a callback, the enigmatic man's cough echoes loudly. He props himself up and assumes a sitting position. She, apprehensive of potential danger, hesitates to make a move, frozen in place. To her surprise, the man stays still without any signs of movement. Spotting a golf club nearby, she cautiously picks it up, mustering her courage as she proceeds to face the man. When the mysterious man notices her in a daze, he asks for a drink of water.

'Water. Can I have some water, please?' The gentle voice and demeanor of the mysterious man, along with his vulnerability, ease her fear. She hurries into the kitchen to fetch him some water. Upon her return, she finds him still sitting with his eyes closed, appearing fragile and non-threatening. Despite this, she remains cautious, prodding him gently with the golf club.

'Hey, here's your water.' She sets it on the table, then takes a step back, keeping a reasonable distance. The mysterious man eagerly seizes the water and drinks it down until the glass is empty.

'Thank you.' Says the mysterious man. He looks at her face with a sense of curiosity, then turns his gaze to the unfamiliar surroundings of the house.

'Where am I?'

'My place.' She replies with an air of indifference, displaying no eagerness to exchange words with him.

'How do I get here?'

'Didn't you know?'

'No.'

'You just had an accident. Got hit by a car.' The mysterious man gazes at her curiously and asks.

'Do I know you? I don't recognize you.'

'No.'

The enigmatic man, overcome by a pulsating ache in his head, reflexively reaches up to relieve the pain, only to see blood on his palms.

'Can you help me get to the hospital?'

'Well, unfortunately, there isn't a hospital around. I meant there is, but quite a distance away. Just wait for my husband. He'll take you.' The enigmatic person gives a placid nod, unconcerned by the oncoming events.

'By the way, I can give you some initial wound care.' She rushes back into the kitchen, collecting makeshift items like a basin of warm water and supplies from the medicine cabinet. She starts by delicately cleansing his face with a damp cloth, displaying both skill and care and trying to engage him in conversation to get to know him better and begin with popular questions.

'What's your name?'

'Uh,. I don't.. I can't remember.' She is convinced that this man has likely experienced a psychological impact regarding his memory. As they both exist in quiet and enveloping silence, the enigmatic man unintentionally gazes at her for an extended period, causing her to feel uneasy and oppressed.

'Could you please stop staring at me?'

'Oh, I'm sorry. I was just trying to figure out if we'd met before, you know. You're... incredibly beautiful.' The enigmatic man admires without intention or the desire to court, but rather as a conversation to reconstruct his own memories. However, it noticeably brings her satisfaction.

Nuch attempts to call Twatchai, but she can't reach him. She sits there, gazing out the window, hoping to see her husband return. As hours pass without any sign of him, Nuch, amidst the sweltering heat, decides to take a shower to cool down. The sound of running water, a familiar noise, prompts the enigmatic man, still half-asleep, to wake up. It triggers memories of a special person—a woman! Unable to recall her appearance, he is mesmerized by the soft and gentle cadence of her voice, which weaves a seductive spell, inviting him with a whisper, "Care to join me for a shower?" The sound of her laughter, like the delicate tinkling of bells, lingers in the air, imbuing the atmosphere with a sense of playful allure. And as the alluring scent of a woman envelops him, he is compelled to follow its trail into the bathroom. The enigmatic man stares, captivated, at the silhouette of Nuch standing exposed behind the semi-transparent curtain. A sense of familiarity, recalling moments of standing together under the shower with that special woman. The person, now a mere silhouette behind the shower curtain, seems indistinguishable from the one in his hazy memories. Nuch is aware of the enigmatic man's presence. She doesn't feel any fear, unsure whether it's due to the curtain separating them, the lingering guilt that led to the incident, or the genuine compliments he has given. The enigmatic man continues to gaze at her through the curtain before politely using his hand to trace the fabric, almost as if he's caressing her silhouette. She extends her hand to meet his, and both hands delicately trace each other. Their hands, gliding over each other, eventually become their lips through the shower curtain. Soon enough, she succumbs to the desires within, pulling back the curtain to let him step closer, standing together under the cascading water from the same showerhead. Their lips press together, and their hands intertwine, flesh pressing against flesh without the barrier of the curtain. Before she realizes it, the mysterious man has intimately entered her essence. Both embrace each other, resembling a long-known intimate couple. The enigmatic man serenades, continuously expressing love, not ceasing until she loses herself in another dimension. Every musical instrument crescendos heavily before reaching its climax and gradually fades into a light, blissful echo. Both surrender to the floor in contentment.

'I have a lot of money.' The mysterious man speaks nonchalantly, his gaze fixed on the ceiling. His face is filled with contemplation. He articulates with emphasis, resembling an individual who has regained their memory.

'I remember I'm loaded.' Nuch just lay there, quietly listening.

'I was about to make a deposit...or something.' The young man comes to a halt, triggering a surge of curiosity within Nuch.

'Do you remember where?' He tries to recall, but it seems like his memory is confined to just that extent.

'That's all I can recall.' The sound of the ringing phone in the lounge intensifies. Nuch grabs a small towel, wraps it around herself, and steps out to pick up the call.

'Hello.'

'Hey, babe, really sorry, my battery's dead. Just parked the car in the garage, heading back now.'

'Just take your time, you know, handle your stuff, I mean, come back whenever you're ready.' her intonation undergoes a noticeable change from how it was before. Her husband senses this shift right after she hangs up the call. Before he can proceed to flag down a taxi, he catches the sound of someone calling his name.

'Mr. Twatchai.' As he turns to locate the voice, he discovers Jenjira, a contemporary and fashionable young lady. She is adorned in elegant attire, exuding a radiant and charming smile.

'Hey, Jen!' He speaks the shortened version of Jenjira's name

'Well, well, it has to be you. I recognized you from behind. What brings you to this area?'

'Oh, just brought the car for repairs and maybe doing a bit of shopping.'

'Hmm, you haven't changed a bit.'

'Aw, you too. So, when did you come back? I heard you left for America?'

'Yeah, It's been a while.'

'How many years has it been since we last met?'

'5 years, I guess.' Jen's voice sounds as if they haven't seen each other in a century. Both of them laugh, looking at each other with joyful smiles, happy to have a spontaneous reunion.

'Walk with me.' Jen invites him to take a stroll together.

'Sure.' Both of them walk together amid the bustling traffic noise. The anxiety that had been gnawing at Twatchai earlier is now fading away. He is unable to avert his gaze elsewhere, constantly admiringly looking at her.

'You're looking a lot better, even kind of sexy.'

'For real? You're not too shabby yourself. By the way, you live around here?'

'Actually, I moved to a different province, just sold my house in Bangkok.'

'Oh, really? Are you married?' Twatchai gazes at Jen with a confident smile before answering.

'Well, still waiting for you.'

The condo door opens, and before they can step inside, Twatchai and Jen intertwine, embracing each other tightly. She tosses her handbag aside, and the emotional intensity quickly escalates. He responds with passionate fervor, both vying to undress the other. Jen throws herself, naked, onto the sofa, and just as the atmosphere heats, the sound of a ringing phone interrupts. Twatchai startles, thinking it might be his wife calling. He looks at the number and realizes it's not her, so he gasps and answers the call.

'Hello…'

'I have to delay your queue schedule.'

'Oh, okay. No problem. I still haven't figured anything out yet.' He hastily replies without pausing to listen to any inquiries from Onn. Jen impatiently seizes Twatchai by the neck and pulls him down between her legs, without giving a damn about who he is conversing with or its significance.

'How's the car situation? Did you find a garage?' Unfazed, Onn maintains her steady stream of conversation at the other end, blissfully ignorant of the fact that the phone has slipped from Twatchai's grasp.

CHAPTER FOUR

Nuch is not adept in culinary matters. The most straightforward dish she can handle is an omelet with green onions and tomatoes. The rest of the meal is purchased ready-made from a restaurant. She simply heats it up, and she continues to receive compliments from the mysterious man.

'Lucky to have come across you. The food is really good.'

In the bygone past, she had Twatchai as her initial and sole boyfriend in her romantic journey. Compliments, exclusive to her husband, never grace her ears, and those once uttered gradually dissipate with time. Now, as these words resurface, they breathe life back into the tenderness of her emotions.

'How's the headache? Feeling better?'

'Much better.'

'Any memories coming back?' The man's demeanor shifts instantly as he starts pondering recovering his memory. It's as if he's forced to navigate through a path filled with thick fog. When he doesn't see the way, he shakes himself out of it and turns back to ask about the person responsible for his current state.

'You know who was driving the car that hit me, by any chance?'

'It's Twatchai..' She inadvertently reveals her husband as the driver involved in the accident, and she attempts to awkwardly amend her statement.

'I mean, it's Twatchai, who can give you the answer.'

'I'm feeling excessively envious.'

'Pardon?'

'Jealous that he has a beautiful wife.'

'With sweet talk like that. I bet there are plenty of girls who fall for you.' They both lock eyes. The mysterious man tries to convey a sense of admiration through his gaze, but it seems she is unfazed. She changes the subject immediately.

'Dessert?' The enigmatic man gently seized her wrist as she rose from the table. She was well aware that he was subtly expressing a desire for something other than dessert.

'My husband could arrive home at any moment. I assume you wouldn't want him to find out about us.' She doesn't explicitly forbid it, but she subtly presents a challenge if he dares to explore further.

On another corner of the city, atop the high-rise condominium, Twatchai bids Jenjira farewell with a kiss, concealing a latent sense of anxiety within his heart.

'Call me, okay?' Twatchai nods his head in response instead of using words. As he walks away from the building, he eagerly pulls out his phone, anticipating multiple missed calls from his wife. To his surprise, there were no missed calls at all. Relief replaces anticipation before he turns to hail a taxi.

As the clock nears midnight, Nuch anxiously awaits her husband's return, who has yet to come home. Simultaneously, the mysterious man finds himself engulfed in a whirlwind of self-discovery, as certain memories resurface. A set of numbers. He rises from the sofa, strides towards the phone, and dials the number. The last digit he dialed matches the exact count of the phone number. The phone signal reverberates. Within moments, someone answers at the other end, as if anticipating the call.

'Hello…' The mysterious man, lost in thought, remains uncertain about who picked up the call. Meanwhile, the individual on the other end of the line unravels the mystery of the caller's identity.

'Somdej. I know it's you. Son of a bitch.' Kiti, the person who owns the number he called, has a personal contact that is known to only a few individuals.

'Who is this?' The mysterious man inquires with sincerity.

'Yeah, fuck you. You're dead, man.' Kiti's face resurfaces in the memory of the man who has lost his memory, now identified as Somdej. The image of Kiti pointing a gun at him prompts Somdej to swiftly hang up the phone. Upon entering the house, the taxi's headlights illuminate the surroundings as it approaches. Somdej quickly retreats into the darkness. Meanwhile, Nuch, lying quietly on the second floor, distinctly hears the intense sounds from Kiti's end of the call. The silence of the house enhances the clarity of the conversation. Twatchai, stepping out of the taxi, walks toward the house. At the same time,

Nuch hurries to unlock the front door, opening it for her husband.

'Why is it so dark?' Twatchai reaches for the switch, flooding the room with light. However, the mysterious man is nowhere to be found on the sofa.

Within the opulent confines of the exclusive, first-class condominium, Kiti endeavors to return a call, only to find the phone signal severed.

'Where is he? Can I please speak to him?' Lalil exclaims anxiously, longing for a conversation with Somdej.

'He probably fucking pulled the plug,' Kiti replies.

'Do you finally believe that I had no part in this?' She asserts her innocence.

Lalil, a striking and refined young woman, perches upon the opulent Barbara Barry sofa, her wrists and ankles ensnared by coils of tape. Kiti strides over with purpose, sinking to his knees to release the bonds encircling her wrists. As he completes the task, she extends her leg gracefully, inviting him to free her ankle. Meanwhile, he steals furtive glances at her slender, captivating legs, unable to resist their allure. With the tape finally removed, he delicately lowers her leg to the ground, as though handling a precious artifact from the Ming Dynasty. She ponders the thoughts racing through Kiti's mind as she tenderly massages her wrists, marked by the lingering confinement.

'I'm curious why he chose to call you on your cell phone instead of contacting me.' Her inquiry leaves him flustered, echoing the very question he had longed to pose himself.

In a brief interlude of quiet, they both pause until she gracefully stands and makes her way to the wine cabinet. She carefully selects a bottle of Pichon Longueville and pours it into a glass.

'Care for a glass?' She asks.

'No,' he answers tersely, his face still

brimming with suspicion.

'You can stay over if you want,' she offers.

'I'd better not,' he replies.

"Are you worried that he might return and find us together?" she says with a hint of playful teasing.

'What's between you and me is history, Lalil, and there's no turning back.'

Hey, pal. I wasn't expecting you to sleep with me. I just noticed you seemed tired and wanted to offer some kindness.'

'Tomorrow morning, I have a flight to catch.'

'Where to?'

'Europe, America.' His words are brief and brusque, reflecting his usual demeanor as if he's reluctant to speak while grappling with numerous pressing thoughts.

'I wonder how you are going to find a partner with this workaholic lifestyle of yours?' She questions him, with subtle undertones, about their relationship's demise, attributing it to his lack of time for her. Kiti keeps silent.

'And how many days will you be gone?' She then continues.

'Three weeks.'

'Three weeks! So what are you going to do with him?'

'I'll deal with him when I return.'

'I can help. Why don't you give me the number?' She volunteers.

Kiti's lips curve into a sardonic smile as he detects the disdain in her tone.

'Are you really suggesting I trust someone who's betrayed me? I've had it with both of you.'

As Kiti rises to leave the house, Lalil asks. 'Tell me, what will you do when you encounter him?'

He turns back with a subtle smile, offering no reply as he exits, gently closing the door behind him.

The enigmatic man flees up to the rooftop of the house. The surrounding rural darkness, perched on the mountain, enhances the brilliance of the night sky. The moon, large and luminous, seems closer than reality. The husband and wife ascend cautiously.

'Mr. Somdej.' Nuch doesn't hesitate to call him by the name Somdej. He doesn't respond immediately, as if unsure whether that name belongs to him. Twatchai initiates the greeting first.

'How's it going? You're looking better.'

'Someone is after me, threatening my life and money.' He speaks without specifying his listener.

'Who is it? Is it the person you were talking to on the phone?' She asks.

Somdej is limited in his ability to respond further due to memory constraints.

'God damn, who am I? What have I done wrong?'

Seeing this, she shifts the conversation to a different topic.

'Er, here he is, Twatchai, my husband,

finally home. Hey, listen, why don't we all go inside and talk?' Somdej lingered in that spot, marveling at the serene ambiance of the quiet night.

'Since you're perfectly alright, I'm happy for you.' Twatchai makes an effort to draw him into conversation.

'Honey, this gentleman can't recall anything. He doesn't know who hit him before you found him.' She fabricates a mysterious driver and portrays her husband as a good Samaritan who encountered the situation and saved the man's life.

'Right. I found you and brought you here.'

'He is starting to remember bit by bit that he's wealthy, and someone is pursuing his fortune.' Nuch tries to act as an intermediary, weaving the narrative of one person for the other to follow along.

'Can I stay here tonight until tomorrow.'

'Of course, you can stay for as many days as you need. Better yet, wait until you're back on your feet before taking off.'

'I don't know how to thank you both.' Twatchai is not one to readily welcome strangers into his home, even though his heart may waver. Nevertheless, he has no alternative, as he feels a direct sense of responsibility deep within, and the unwavering support from his wife leaves no room for objections. Thus, he reluctantly yields. Nuch maintains her husband's composure until the enigmatic man vanishes from the rooftop. She delicately inquires about the events of that day.

'Where are his belongings?'

'What belongings?'

'Come on, Wat. He must have had bags, cases, or a sack to carry the money.'

'I saw him carrying nothing.' He answers without a moment's hesitation. It appears to be an answer that doesn't sit well with his beloved one.

'And what about the car? What was he driving?' It appears that she is unwilling to relent in her pursuit of discovering the enigmatic man's belongings. Twatchai feigns contemplation, striving to persuade her that he is making an earnest effort to collaborate.

'I don't know.' His reply further dampens her expectations.

'Why didn't you observe anything at all?'

'What do you expect me to observe? There's nothing there—just trees, and,..uh, wait, there's a gas station.' The memory of the gas station, situated close to the scene of the accident, surfaces vividly in his mind. 'Maybe he stopped to refuel. Yes!'

CHAPTER FIVE

Twatchai pedals his bicycle out of the house in the pre-dawn darkness, making his way toward the gas station with the hope of discovering any potential traces left in that vicinity.

Somdej is getting ready to depart. Nuch brings Twatchai's clothing for him to change into and tries to persuade him to stay.

'You should stay for another day or two, or go to the hospital to have a physical check-up to be sure. It might be better than risking it, don't you think?'

'Thanks a lot, but I'm anxious to go out and discover who I am.'

The mutual intimacy they reveal to each other in the moments when Twatchai is absent. She takes care of him just like any other husband of hers, and she openly tries to express her desires towards him.

'I must be thinking about you.'

'I can't stand seeing you belong to someone else either.' Somdej's own longing for her is not insignificant. However, the torment of having to witness her belonging to Twatchai is substantial. This is the reason he feels compelled to leave, and Nuch, filled with sorrow, cannot bring herself to detain him. She approaches, enveloping him in a tender hug, much like a child unwilling to release its grip on its mother.

'Please stay.' He gently pushes her away from his embrace, denying her attempt to kiss him. As he walks towards the door, he pauses, turning back to meet her defiant gaze. In that moment, she stands boldly, provocatively exposed. Despite his internal struggle, he can't resist the allure of her charm. He returns to her, and they share a passionate embrace and kiss, succumbing to an overwhelming desire until both find satisfaction.

'I have a company... Yeah, I own a company.' In the tranquil moments of repose, Somdej's memories slowly resurface. She turns her gaze towards him, lending a supportive ear.

'A company?'

'That's all I can recall.'

'What color? The building?'

Somdej shifts his attention, locking eyes with the young woman radiating a joyful smile beside him. The flirtatious twinkle in her gaze, an endless allure, seamlessly entwines with his own.

'My memory comes back every time we make love. I reckon it needs another go.' He speaks with a playful yet sincere tone, evoking laughter from her. Together, they embark on the next chapter of their romantic adventure.

Twatchai, fatigued and breathing heavily, arrives at the gas station after cycling. Glancing around, he observes an absence of parked cars—not a single one in sight. Straining to peer into the distance, he discerns only trees. The distant bell resonates with a gentle melody. It's only at this moment that he realizes there's a temple nearby, though it appears too far from the scene of the incident to harbor any hope of discovering evidence. He walks into the convenience store at the gas station, grabs a bottle of water, and sits down to rest near the front. He picks up a newspaper left on the table and starts reading to pass the time. As he flips through the pages, he comes across a photo of Somdej in the business section. Below the image, there is a caption that reads, "Wanted for arrest... Somdej. Embezzled over 100 million from the company."

CHAPTER SIX

In the summertime on the mountaintop, the weather is delightful, unlike other parts of the region. The wife and her paramour, ascend to sit on the rooftop, enjoying the comfortable air while savoring local wine. She wears Twatchai's oversized shirt with just a few buttons fastened, and snug shorts that emphasize her toned legs, as if intentionally flaunting her enticing charm throughout the time. After a prolonged exchange, they eventually reach the juncture, which Somdej is eager to explore.

'Share your story with me?'

'What do you want to know?'

'Anything, something memorable.'

'You already know every piece of me.' She is deliberately trying to playfully provoke him rather than responding to the questions, while Somdej is keen on learning more about Nuch beyond what he already knows.

'How did you and Twatchai meet?' Nuch noticed that he wasn't in the mood to engage playfully, and she earnestly turned to respond.

'There's nothing remarkable in my life. After graduating as a nurse, I met him on my first day of work.'

'Can't believe you graduated as a nurse.'

'Why's that?'

'You just don't seem to fit in this profession.'

'Realized I chose the wrong major when I started working.'

'Why's that?'

'Dealing with blood and being around sick people all day every day. I could only handle it for a week before resigning.'

'But being a nurse is a noble profession.'

'I admit those who become nurses must be willing to make real sacrifices.'

'I would love to see you dressed as a nurse. It must look sexy.'

Nuch's husband arrives home filled with excitement, catching snippets of his wife's conversation with the other man on the rooftop. The subtle return of her husband leaves her feeling a bit shaken. She endeavors to conceal her unease with tender and sweet words.

'Oh, you're back. Can I get a kiss?' Twatchai stands motionless, unyielding to his wife's request for a kiss upon his return. To diffuse the underlying tension in their relationship, Somdej interjects, praising the scenic beauty around them.

'The view is absolutely stunning, isn't it?' Twatchai grapples with a dilemma more captivating than the suspicions arising from his wife's association with the stranger right in front of him. He holds the belief that the contents within his grasp possess the capability to address and resolve the challenges. Striving to mask his resentment, he beckons for his wife to accompany him.

'Nuch, come with me. I have something I want to show you.'

Twatchai, guiding his wife with a gentle tug, steps out onto the backyard lawn. He then unfolds a newspaper for her to peruse. After the truth is unveiled, her emotions undergo an immediate transformation.

'Now it all makes sense.'

'I'll go to the police.'

'Wait, why don't we negotiate for a share?'

'This is a crime, honey.'

'No one knows he's here. And you've destroyed all the evidence, haven't you?' Her proposition causes him to hesitate, pondering the colossal benefits that no one dares to refuse. Nevertheless, he can't envision a path or a lawful means to acquire that disliked property.

'What if he refuses to share?'

'That's when we go to the cop.'

'And if he bolts, what can we do?' The challenging question he throws back at Nuch gives her something to contemplate. As always, she finds a solution and responds to her husband promptly.

'Well, he seems a bit out of it at the moment. First, we need to figure out where the money is. I'll try to get him to disclose the hiding spot, and then we can decide our next steps. Maybe we won't even have to split it with him.' The final words uttered by the wife seem more decisive than the tenderness he has known from her throughout the years. This increasingly obscures any potential avenue for him to acquire that fortune.

'How do you plan to do that?'

'Just leave it to me. I'll handle it.' In no time, she transforms into a person full of confidence in her plan. Twatchai, a skilled writer accustomed to carefully considering each sentence before putting pen to paper, acknowledges the flexibility of the writing process, where one can discard and rewrite. In contrast, real life lacks the luxury of revisiting and correcting mistakes. Nevertheless, his beloved wife remains steadfast, prepared to face challenges with confidence. He steps back, enabling her to showcase her skills, albeit with a hint of concern.

'Be cautious not to make him aware. Pretend you're clueless.'

Twatchai strolls with his wife, ascending once more to the rooftop. Somdej, on the other hand, revels in the familiar ambiance. Greeting both of them with a subtly altered demeanor and playfully making remarks.

'Where have y'all been? Look like you've seen a ghost.' Both of them feign laughter.

'The wire.' Twatchai's remark hangs in the air, casting a veil of confusion over Nuch and Somdej, both struggling to decipher its meaning.

'The telephone wire was cut.'

Somdej, understanding the implication, chooses to remain silent, while Nuch remains bewildered.

'What are you talking about, babe?

'In this household of three, someone amongst us has severed the wire. I'm curious as to the motive behind it.'

Somdej grapples with the realization that he's the one who severed the telephone wire, his memory loss adding to the complexity of the situation. The unsettling conversation over the phone had triggered fear within him, ultimately leading to his decision to cut the line that day. Now, he finds himself at a loss for words, unsure of how to articulate the truth to Twatchai in a manner that he would comprehend.

'It's about time. I should leave.' He seeks his escape through the act of bidding farewell.

'Don't go just yet.' Nuch's reply is swift, met with the immediate support of her husband.

'Right, the party isn't over yet.'

'This is the love nest of the married couple. I don't want to intrude.'

'No need to feel that way. It's my responsibility that I crashed into you.' The brewing resentment harbored by his wife and her discontent in the company of the enigmatic man sparked a momentary surge of malice within him, compelling him to unleash his wrath and expose the truth, stirring a sense of urgency in Nuch, who must promptly address the situation.

'It was an accident, you know.'

'Indeed, you crossed in front of my car, and I couldn't brake in time.' Somdej couldn't figure out how the actual incident occurred. If it's a genuine accident, he has no right to blame Twatchai or anyone. However, the peculiar behavior of this couple makes him suspicious. He can't be sure whether it's a real accident or not. He shifts his gaze towards the surroundings, attempting to reassure himself of his physical well-being, contemplating a positive perspective.

'Fortunately, I'm unharmed, physically.'

'Please accept my apologies.' Despite his inner dissatisfaction with his wife, Somdej endeavors to preserve the aspirations she has set for herself.

'I don't hold any grudges or blame you. Your wife took care of me so well that I don't know how to repay her kindness.' In the depths of his being, Somdej conceals feelings for Nuch. He speaks with a certain nuance, providing her with a glimpse, even if it involves being sharp about her relationship with her husband. His gaze remains fixed on the lady, refusing to shy away. Nuch, in this moment, is somewhat perplexed, especially as she unravels the intricate complexities of this enigmatic stranger.

'Stay. Let us take care of you until your memory returns, and then you can decide where to go.'

'Where do you plan to go?'

'Honestly, I'm clueless. I can't even picture what my mother looks like. Meeting her without being able to greet her properly would just add to the confusion.' Somdej's response injects a touch of humor, easing the tension that had arisen among the three individuals.

As the evening sky darkens, the lingering melancholy still clings to Twatchai's heart. He sips on wine to drown his sorrows. Meanwhile, he awakens his passionate feelings towards his wife. Nuch sits brushing her hair in front of the mirror, preparing to retire for the night. Twatchai stands admiring the beauty of his wife through the mirrored reflection, his solid, firm piece of flesh rubbing on her back. He offers her a sip of wine from his glass. He inhales the scent of her neck and ears before lightly kissing her lips. The subtle sound of their interactions reaches the other man, who lies below. Unable to escape the awareness of what this couple is doing, Somdej discreetly ascends the stairs.

His gaze aligns with the floor of the second level, allowing him to witness the husband and wife undressing and embracing on the bed, indulging in an intimate moment.

The husband rocks back and forth for a few moments before reaching the climax. He collapses as if he has been playing sports for several hours, lying down beside his wife, who's about to feel amorous.

'Honey, I'll make it up for you next time.' The phrase she often hears after having intimate moments with her dreamy husband. She lies bare, embracing the coolness of the air conditioner, feeling completely abandoned. At this moment, she has learned how the sexual differences between the two men manifest. Before long, the husband, now snoring, blends seamlessly with the soft hum of the air conditioner's breeze. She grabs a cover-up, puts it on, and rises from the bed to head to the bathroom. The moment her feet touch the first floor of the house, she senses the boundary of another man whose gaze is fixed on her at this particular juncture. Both of them lock eyes with an intensity that doesn't waver, not allowing their gazes to stray. The young man can't resist moving closer, akin to a predator locking onto prey entering its territory. He approaches without making physical contact or reaching out to touch her. The person who feels trembling turns out to be Nuch herself, feeling a pervasive warmth throughout her body. He leans in, drawing close, and she tilts her chin to reveal her lips, anticipating a kiss from him. However, he pulls back, teasingly avoiding her. Then, the stud leans in again, this time near her ear, whispering softly.

'The pleasure you desire is right in front of you. Why hesitate?' Nuch, overcome with eagerness, felt a shiver down her spine as she tried to kiss him. However, Casanova intentionally dodged her advances, playfully teasing her. She responds provocatively.

'It's your imagination running wild,

thinking that I desire you.'

'Your eyes are demanding, seeking me out all the time. I can tell.' The pair, in close proximity, engage in what could be termed a breath-to-breath encounter, inhaling deeply but refraining from physical contact. Both playfully provoke and are provoked. As the sexy beast attempts to escalate, She retreats until her back meets the wall. The playful games cease when they share a passionate kiss, completely absorbed in each other's presence, succumbing to the intoxication of their profound connection. The lingering tension from a moment ago in Nuch transforms into the desired happiness she yearns for. She even exclaims in abandon, momentarily forgetting herself, as they reach the pinnacle of ecstasy.

Twatchai awakens abruptly, realizing it's a new morning. His beloved is nowhere to be found in bed. The haunting echoes of her wailing pierce the air, prompting him to spring out of bed in a frantic search for his love. An unsettling stillness envelops the room, and the mysterious man is conspicuously absent from the sofa where he should be. Something must have transpired. He dashes in a frenzied quest for the couple, yet they elude his sight. Hastening back upstairs, he seizes a pair of binoculars, scanning the distance in a desperate attempt to unravel the unfolding mystery.

The wife and her paramour discreetly linger behind the trees. Somdej subtly discerns the hidden silhouette of his rival and realizes that he's probably aiming binoculars their way. The man seems to be growing suspicious of the pair.

'Where is he?'

'Don't turn around. I see him with binoculars. Act like we're out for a stroll.'

The duo emerges from the shelter of the tree, simulating a casual stroll for exercise. Twatchai descends quickly, meeting them as they return to the house.

'You were sleeping like a baby, so we thought

it best not to disturb you.' Somdej endeavors to speak for Nuch. Twatchai, reluctant to engage in conversation with him, seizes Nuch's arm with a touch of irritation in his tone.

'What do you think you're doing?'

'Taking him for a walk. Speed up his recovery, you know that.' It's an answer that leaves Twatchai with no room for further doubts about her.

CHAPTER SEVEN

Twatchai's emotional state mirrors the congestion of Bangkok's traffic. Upon collecting his repaired car, he seizes the chance to visit the contemporary and stylish Jenjira. Welcoming him with a sweet smile. She remains in her undergarments, preparing to attire herself for an outing. She discerns the countenance of her lover, who is melancholic and pensive.

'Hey, Wat, come in. What's wrong? You look sad.'

'Nah, nothing. Just thinking of you.'

'Aw, I think of you too. I miss you too.' She speaks in a blend of Thai and English, reminiscent of Thais who have experienced life abroad. Twatchai makes a move to embrace her, but she tactfully restrains herself.

'No, no, no. I'm about to pick up a friend at the airport.'

'Perfect timing. My car has just been repaired. I can give you a ride?'

'Oh, no need. It's sort of personal.' Twatchai's noble intentions are outright dismissed.

'Alright then, I'll wait here.'

'Sorry. Um, it's just that Peter is coming from America. If he meets you, it might not go well.' He falls into a brief stunned silence upon hearing the name Peter.

'Who the heck is Peter?' He is aware that Peter is a male name, but his curiosity extends beyond that. He never considered the possibility that his covert partner might have someone else beside him. Caught off guard, Jen herself doesn't know how to conceal it and straightforwardly confides in Twatchai.

'He's my boyfriend.'

'I see.' Twatchai attempts a smile, masking the lingering disappointment. Before he takes his leave.

'Wait, can you write down your new address for me, please?'

'Yeah, sure.' He strides out of the room, seemingly adrift in a world of his own, detached from the vibrant surroundings. He meanders along the bustling street, yet an overwhelming solitude pervades his being. It's as if his heart, already fractured, undergoes further fractures. Despite his initial resolve to open up to Jen, the emotional weight appears to deepen, pressing upon him with greater intensity than before.

When the husband is away, the house transforms into a haven for the clandestine affair between the paramour and the young wife. The rhythmic echoes of high heels reverberate against the floor, heightening the curiosity of Somdej. As Nuch appears in a form-fitting nurse outfit, accentuated by white stockings that enhance her allure, the paramour gazes with desire, eagerly advancing towards her. Their passion unfolds within the confines of every corner, and every inch of the household becomes a paradise for the couple. Each encounter reaches its zenith, etching vivid memories for Somdej, only to be revisited bit by bit.

'Kiti, that son of a bitch business partner of mine, has betrayed me.' Embarking on her initial foray into intimacy, she explores, driven by curiosity and sheer enjoyment. The thrill of a covert rendezvous evolves into shared and indelible impressions. As the stakes rise to involve finances, Nuch commits to a romantic involvement with Somdej, aiming to reconstruct his memories and ultimately gain financial rewards.

'Where's the money?'

And it's a response that eludes Somdej, buried deep within the recesses of his memories.

'Money?' It has transformed into a responsibility that she must diligently carry out until it is excavated from the recesses of his memories.

Twatchai drives back with a heart adrift. He feels despondent during this time of solitude and sorrow. Upon his return, he dedicates himself to earnestly writing his book, drawing inspiration from real events in his home. He crafts characters from his sexy wife and a mysterious man, intertwining the imaginative images seamlessly with real occurrences. Stimulating emotions such as anger, hatred, envy, love, and jealousy, he records a powerful epic in this novel.

Working day and night without leaving home, the clandestine lovers couple miss the chance to get close to each other. They can only exchange glances. But then one day, supplies are running low. Twatchai's duty requires him to drive into town to bring home essential items. Dressed in his casual attire, he descends the stairs to where the couple is relaxing at opposite ends of the house.

'I'm heading to town to grab some stuff. You guys need anything?'

The profound stillness serves as their response, both engrossed in their current activities, diverting more attention to their immediate tasks than to Twatchai's inquiry. He conceals his suspicions, keeping them undisclosed, ensuring that neither of them can apprehend it, before leaving the house with bitterness.

The resonance of the diesel engine gradually diminishes, drifting farther away until it fades into the serene distance. An unspoken accord between the illicit couple triggers their simultaneous ascent, entwining them in an embrace that envelops them in warmth and intimacy.

Twatchai steers the car along a winding

downhill path, abruptly halting and swiftly exiting the vehicle. He ascends through a shortcut in the dense, thorny forest. His heart races, not due to physical exertion but fueled by the vivid images in his imagination that elicit excitement. Meanwhile, the extramarital couple, reunited after several days, passionately embraces and shares kisses. As the husband reaches the door, forcefully pushing it open, he creates a startling tableau for his wife and her clandestine lover. Startled, each of them jumps away, heading in opposite directions. The husband lunges forward, delivering a punch to Somdej's face, sending him to the ground. Nuch's screams reverberate through the house, denouncing any escalation of violence.

'No, Wat, stop.' Twatchai's countenance reveals a blend of anger and revenge as he quickly grabs the hidden gun from the cabinet, pointing it threateningly at the adulterer's head. This moment triggers memories for Somdej, reminiscent of a past incident when he faced a similar threat from Kiti and involuntarily released a loud plea.

'Don't shoot. Alright, I will return all the money.' Nuch is taken aback by the sudden revelation from her paramour. Undaunted, she advances, delivering a resounding slap across his face, determined to extract the answers she seeks. From her perspective, she intends to convey to her husband that her connection with this man is solely a quest to uncover his hidden wealth, not a covert affair.

'Where's the money?'

'What money? I don't know. I can't remember. You know damn well, I can't remember anything.' The intensified emotions elevate her acting, rendering her portrayal even more authentically in line with her intentions.

'Don't try to play off your forgetfulness. I've been suspicious since day one.' She alludes to the evening when Somdej contacted Kiti, a discussion she clandestinely eavesdropped on from the house's second floor. If he couldn't recall anything, how did he manage to get Kiti's phone number? This forms the basis of her skepticism regarding his memory. She retrieves the evidence, presenting the phone bill to him for inspection.

'Kiti's number, the partner you manipulated to extract money. Don't try to make me look foolish.' Somdej burst into laughter upon hearing her accusations, looking at her with disbelief that she could change from a sweet young woman to a defiant and assertive woman. Nuch's gaze intensifies with anger towards him. She snatches the gun from her husband and points it menacingly at his head.

'Tell me where you hid the money now, or I will blow your brains out.'

'Ooh, I'm scared. You wouldn't dare pull the trigger. If I die, you won't gain anything either... You're no different from that scoundrel Kiti, hungry for money.'

Amid the escalating tension, the faint voice of a woman resonates from the outside.

'Hello... Is anyone home?' It's Jen! As she swiftly enters the house, all eyes turn toward her. Jenjira is taken aback by the frozen expressions on everyone's faces, each one caught in an unusual tableau. She can only manage a sheepish smile.

'Are you guys shooting a movie?'

'What do you want?' The unexpected guest points her finger provocatively at Twatchai. Nuch shifts her gaze towards her husband, her eyes filled with doubts concerning whether he is secretly involved with another woman. Twatchai swiftly conceals the smile he shares with Jenjira.

'May I come in?'

'As you wish.' The inviting tone in Nuch's voice lacks a certain warmth, making Jenjira reluctant to make a move. She remains poised near the entrance of the house, anticipating a more inviting gesture from Twatchai. Opting for a wave to greet him, in turn, he responds with a simple raised hand in acknowledgment.

'Aren't you going to introduce us?' All lies within the unwavering gaze of his wife, an inevitability one cannot elude. Consequently, the husband finds himself compelled to elegantly shift the focus back to Somdej.

'Hey, where's the goddamn money?'

'How many times do I have to repeat myself that I don't remember?' Twatchai approached and retrieved the concealed newspaper, casting it onto the floor before the amnesiac person.

'Maybe this will help jog your memory... the authorities have issued a countrywide arrest warrant. A sum exceeding 100 million Baht, wow, man.'

Jen exclaimed, 'Wow, camera! Where's the camera?' Jen fades from everyone's attention. A lawful wife, however, persists with her original inquiry, underscoring it once more.

'I'm going to ask you one more time, where is the money?'

'Even in a tough situation, you're proving to be resilient. Didn't realize you were as adept as you are in bed.' She employed the gun to strike Somdej's face, prompting him to turn in reaction to the impact. Jen, now, discerned that this was far from a casual scenario.

'Oh, my god. I'll come back another time.'

'Hold your horses, what exactly is your business here?' Nuch gracefully approached, closing the distance between herself and Jenjira.

'Um, I just dropped by to see Wat, that's all.'

'I suppose your objective here is to fuck him.'

'Gosh, you're rude!' Twatchai notices the potential for his wife to inadvertently cause harm to Jenjira, prompting him to quickly stride over and intervene.

Nuch uses the muzzle to lift a spaghetti strap on Jenjira's camisole, causing the tied knot to loosen and revealing a glimpse of her breast. Jenjira quickly pulls the knot back into place.

'Adorned as if ready-to-eat instant noodles,

just a rip of the packet, and she's good to go.'

'Stop it. You're insulting her.'

'Care to bet? Nothing underneath there.' Nuch glides the gun's muzzle down to the hem of the skirt, seductively raising the fabric to expose the bare skin underneath, with no underwear. In the poignant exchange of feminine emotions, as both women reveal traces of jealousy towards the same man, Somdej seizes the opportune moment with a poised leap through the rear window. Jenjira, directing her gaze towards the escape route, urgently calls out to inform the spouses.

'He's gone.' Somdej sprints towards the front of the house, where Jenjira's car rests. In one fluid motion, he vaults into the waiting vehicle and accelerates away, eluding the pursuit of the three others.

'No, no, no, not my car.' Jenjira shouts out loudly. In a hurried dash, Twatchai descends the shortcut leading to his parked car nestled by the roadside. Upon arriving at his vehicle, a disheartening revelation awaits him—all four tires have been deliberately deflated.

Kiti, returning to Suvarnabhumi Airport, is taken aback to discover Lalil awaiting his arrival.

"I told your driver that I'd come to pick you up myself,"

Her action leaves him unsatisfied.

'Very well then, here, take my luggage and carry to the car'

As Lalil's eyes fall upon the expansive travel bag, she can't help but feel a pang of reluctance. She's not the type of woman meant for such physical tasks, a fact she silently reaffirms within herself. Though she begins to voice her protest, a sense of hesitation washes over her, a recognition of the calculated ploy he's employing to provoke her, regardless of his motives. With a resigned sigh, she extends her hand towards the bag's handle, preparing to drag it. But before she can even make contact, he releases her grip, leaving her momentarily baffled by his sudden change of heart.

'This matter is between me and Somdej. None of your business.' Kiti's words aim to sever her from any further entanglement.

'What are you going to do with him?' Her outward motive revolves around care and concern, yet her covert intentions remain shrouded in secrecy, known to none.

'I suggest it's best for you to move on. That son of a bitch has never been genuinely in love with anyone. I had cautioned you about this, but you've never taken my advice."

As Kiti's words trailed off, he retrieved his travel bag and departed, leaving Lalil in a state of numb silence.

The once tumultuous events settle down as Somdej departs, leaving a residue of emotional turbulence for the newlyweds, especially impacting the lawful husband, who undergoes a transformation. The love he once lavished upon his ideal wife morphs into profound disdain. Despite her attempts to reconnect with him, extending her heart, he remains indifferent. Twatchai's once fervent desires evolve into lingering bitterness. Seated before the computer screen day and night, he seeks solace in closing the novel scripted from the bitter realities that unfold in real-life events.

'Still mad at me?' She inquires with a tender voice, weighed down by her own sense of wrongdoing.

'I need concentration for my work.' Her remorseful tone fails to bring about any positive change. His demeanor suggests a reluctance to unlock the door to rekindle ties with her. In a surprising turn of events, he makes an unexpected decision, opting to reach out to Onn through a phone call.

'Hello, Onn. Do you still have an interest in purchasing my property?'

'I'm not in the mood for jokes right now.'

'No, I mean it.' Onn gently withdraws her hand from the stack of documents spread across the table. A contemplative air envelops her as she is stirred by the genuine and weighty tone of Twatchai's voice. Within the depths of that tone lingers an undertone of anger, a subtle resonance veiled in complex emotions. It is this very anger that serves as the driving force propelling Twatchai to reach a decision—to dismantle and abandon the once cherished honeymoon house.

'Well, let's meet up in a couple of days.'

Nuch was acutely aware of the seismic decision her husband had just made, and as she beheld the disintegration of everything around her, she traced it back to the vulnerability of her own heart. It all commenced with a yearning to venture into an intimate connection with a stranger. Gradually, that exploration metamorphoses into a profound entanglement—an irresistible allure that defies moral and righteous boundaries. Ultimately, the repercussions eclipse every ethical consideration. In the end, secrets, no matter how carefully guarded, unravel, leading to a day of dissolution. On the contrary, she harbors no reproach toward Twatchai for his covert romantic entanglements. If this were to become a matter of dispute, it would likely result in separation, a conclusion she desperately wishes to evade. She stands there, casting her gaze once again upon the enchanting house atop the beautiful hill, an overwhelming sense of remorse gripping her. Unbeknownst to her, tears cascade down her cheeks, an unrestrained and poignant release. In the vast expanse of her emotions, a small ember of hope glows, akin to an oasis in the endless desert. She envisions a future moment when his anger dissipates, and on that day, she pledges to transform herself into the epitome of the ideal wife he never knew he needed. For now, she patiently awaits the arrival of that transformative day.

CHAPTER EIGHT

Amidst the bustling heart of Bangkok's central business district, Chai, the driver strides into the CEO's opulent office located in a towering skyscraper. With purposeful steps, he approaches Kiti, presenting him with a document procured from the telecommunications corporation.

'Boss, I've got the address of the house and the name of the owner.' the driver informs.

'Good job, Chai.'

As Chai makes a move to leave the room,

Kiti asks him. 'Wait, I have a favor to ask.'

'Yes, boss'

'Could you help me rent a car?'

'Um, yeah?' Chai found himself puzzled as to why his boss would require a rented car when he already possessed a fleet of vehicles at his disposal.

The boss continues 'I need a family-sized one, nothing too big, and preferably with tinted windows. The darker the better.' Kiti's words trickle out gradually, each sentence carefully crafted as he articulates his thoughts. He observed the furrowed brow on Chai's face, a telltale sign of suspicion. Desperate to conceal his true intentions, he concocted a fabricated tale to deceive his driver.

'I'm renting it for a friend.' Chai's lingering suspicion prompts him to inquire.

'Um, which class of car would you prefer, sir?'

'Just a regular car, nothing too fancy'

'Does it have to be a Mercedes?'

'No need, this friend of mine is from upcountry.' The mention of "upcountry" makes it easier for Chai to understand what kind of car he should look for.

'I see.'

'One more thing, don't mention this to anyone. You know, personal thing.' He subtly signals his driver with a wink.

'Right. Which days are we looking at?'

'Tomorrow, through the weekend.'

'Yes, boss'

The insistent rap on the door reverberates, prompting Jenjira to stride towards it. Opening the door, she witnesses the uninvited guest making a self-assured entrance. As he removes his cap, Jenjira's recognition ignites an immediate surge of anger within her.

'It's you. Give me back my car?'

Somdej twirls the car key ring on his index finger to catch her attention. She eagerly reaches out to grab them, but with a swift and deft motion, he pulls them just out of her reach.

'I'm going to call the cops.'

'I've brought your car over. How about sharing a cup of coffee as a gesture of appreciation?' His voice resonates without a hint of malice, casting her into a state of hesitation about her next move.

'Come on, be nice, and I'll leave.' She moves aside, allowing him to enter the guest reception area. As he strolls through the space, his eyes wander, exploring the surroundings. Suddenly, a captivating image captures his attention—an exquisite photograph showcasing Jenjira smiling before the iconic Statue of Liberty in New York. Somdej's eyes subtly shift toward Jenjira, who stands still, scrutinizing him with a gaze that reveals a lack of trust.

'Where's my coffee?'

'I don't have it. I ran out.' He grinned, sensing her reluctance to brew him a cup of coffee. Meanwhile, she senses that he harbors intentions beyond merely enjoying a cup of coffee.

'What exactly is it that you want?'

'Now we are talking. I need a place to lay low.'

'You're practically suggesting I end up behind bars.'

'I'm willing to pay.' Financial matters tend to weave their way through every situation, particularly for unemployed beauties like Jen, who have no intention of seeking employment but desire a life of comfort and ease.

'How much?' His gaze drifted once more to the photograph of Jenjira standing before the Statue of Liberty, a longing he believed she harbored for a return visit. Without hesitation, he extended an offer.

'America.' Jenjira replies with a derisive tone, mocking the invaluable terms he has set.

'Bull shit. I don't give a damn about America. I can go whenever I want.' Her scornful words make it clear to him that she possesses both the means and the resources to venture on her own. Thus, he raises the stakes for the bet. 'It's a big difference being there as a waitress or being the owner of the restaurant.' She takes a moment to contemplate before elegantly settling into the chair across. With finesse, she presents the ultimate offer she has envisioned.

'10 mil.' Somdej chuckled lightly under his breath, his laughter pregnant with concealed nuances.

'Fine, but it has to include everything, all-inclusive.'

'What do you mean, what everything?' Jen's voice resonates with sincerity, poised to reject the deal if it falls short of her satisfaction. Somdej, left with no alternative, approaches, seeking a means to inspire her.

'10 million seems a bit steep, but I don't mind paying if everything aligns with my terms. You're still young and have opportunities ahead of you. This money could turn things around for you. Think about it. The deal will end the moment I walk out of this room.'

Jenjira eases her bare form onto her bedding, accentuating the soft contours of her rounded bosom. Somdej, maintaining a calm demeanor, tenderly explores her with a composed passion, savoring each unfolding moment, an investment of time that proves undeniably worthwhile. He let out a triumphant shout in sync with the climax.

'The money is in the car.'

'Where's the car?

'I can't remember where I parked it.'

'Try harder. What if someone finds it and takes it?'

'I might as well need another round.'

The car, its windows darkened to conceal the occupants within, glides to a stop and parks gracefully in front of a quaint roadside shop. Kiti, stepping out with purpose, makes his way into the store, intent on unraveling the mystery surrounding the house he's traced from a phone number. Inside, the shop owner offers little solace, explaining that house numbers in this area follow a chronological order of construction rather than the conventional cardinal directions. Disheartened by the lack of clarity, Kiti emerges from the shop, his expression etched with genuine frustration. He casts a searching gaze around the surroundings aimlessly. The shop owner approaches him after realizing something.

'I just recall there are a couple of settlers who moved here from Bangkok. It might be the house you're looking for.'

In the midst of the rhythmic dance of the keyboard and the nightly symphony, Twatchai remains entranced by the glow of his screen, typing away ceaselessly. Unaware of the solitude enveloping his wife, Nuch's thoughts drift back to the moments of joy she once shared with her paramour. She contemplates the enigma of what society deems right, questioning why adherence to correctness often falls short of bringing true contentment. The very righteousness, when upheld, is met with disapproval, leaving her pondering the intricacies of life's moral tapestry.

Both remain oblivious to the fact that they are currently within Kiti's vigilant purview. Kiti, concealed within his car behind tinted windows, covertly observes the scene from a distance, seamlessly blending into the shadows of the night. With unwavering determination, he exits the vehicle and strides purposefully towards Twatchai's residence. Meanwhile, inside the brightly lit interior, starkly contrasting with the darkness outside, the boundary between visibility and obscurity is starkly delineated. Despite Kiti's thorough inspection, his search for Somdej yields no results, unbeknownst to him that Somdej had left the premises before his arrival. Undeterred, Kiti decides to dial Somdej's recent call number, the ring echoing through the tranquil night. Moments later, he notices Nuch approaching to answer the call.

'Hello.' She answers softly. He chooses silence, preferring to observe the scene unfolding before him. Meanwhile, Nuch pulls the phone cord nearer to the window, bringing her face into clear view for him, who watches intently from his vantage point.

'Is that you?' Nuch whispers discreetly, ensuring her husband doesn't overhear. In the depths of her contemplation, she realizes the importance of maintaining a cool demeanor, lest it stir further discord between her and her spouse. Yet, against this rational notion, she opts to delve into conversation with him, driven by a perplexing curiosity about the purpose behind his call. Kiti holds his silence, clutching the phone line as he observes intently, while she persists in her refusal to disconnect, steadfast in her belief that the other end is no one but her ex-lover. Her countenance betrays a mounting restlessness.

'Hello, Hello.' Her voice grows louder as she whispers. Twatchai exclaims, 'Who's calling?' Uncertain whether the whispered conversation is reaching his ears.

'Nobody.' Swiftly places the phone back down. Kiti harbors the belief that he's landed at the correct abode, despite the absence of the figure he wanted most. Observations coupled with his intimate knowledge of his partner's character traits lead him to firmly believe in Somdej's imminent return.

In the hush of a tranquil morning at the diminutive, abandoned gas station, a sleek black car glides in. Somdej unlatches the door, steps out, and scans the area, attempting to summon the memories of his inaugural visit. He endeavors to discern any subtle cues that might rekindle recollections of the car he once steered. Yet, the specifics—make, model, or color—elude him, veiled behind the ethereal mist.

Despite the challenging circumstances, Nuch puts in her utmost effort to be a loving wife. She remains dedicated to her exercise routine, ensuring she maintains her physique. Should the day come when her relationship with her husband concludes, she is prepared to embark on a new chapter of love without hesitation. As she returns home, an unexpected surprise awaits, quietly nestled inside. The unusual stillness wraps around her as she enters the pathway, an eerie departure from the customary symphony of keyboard clicks or the melodious tunes that usually accompany Twatchai's creative endeavors. Her steps echo in the hush as she crosses the threshold, and there, once again, sits Somdej on the sofa. A twist of surprise grips her as she finds her husband, Twatchai, bound to a chair, his hands securely tied. In Somdej's hand, a gun and a smile are gracing his lips as he greets her.

'Step in, beautiful. So we can have a complete assembly. Take a seat.' The beautiful figure hesitates, her gestures uncertain and bewildering. The perplexity painted across her face mirrors her internal struggle to decipher how she should respond to the unfolding.

'Can't decide, huh? Does he still love you?

Hey, Wat, do you still love your wife? Only silence from the husband.

'I tell you what, sweetie. Come sit with me.' His hand landed on the seat next to him with a deliberate thud, a visual proclamation of the dominance he wielded over all. Nuch, regaining her poise, chose to surrender herself to a chair at a distance.

'You need not worry about him. Do you know why? Because he plans to abandon you anyway.' Somdej shifted his gaze towards Twatchai, directing the probing question towards him.

'Am I right, Wat? If you don't want her, then I'll take her.'

'I hate you.' His former paramour speaks with a venomous tongue, her voice laden with resentment and simmering anger.

'But I love you.' Somdej's words cast a veil of uncertainty over whether he speaks from a sincere heart or harbors a subtle intention to mock this married couple.

'That's my first agenda. As for the second agenda, I've come to retrieve the keys to my car. That's all. Meeting adjourned.'

'I told you, he has a car.' Once again, she asserts clearly to Twatchai.

'I've looked everywhere, and there's not a single car in that area.'

'You're of no help. That's why you never accomplish anything.' Nuch seizes the opportune moment to blame her husband for the collapse of their relationship, oblivious to the potential impact her words might have on his professional passion. An undercurrent of anger courses through him, leading to an immediate retort.

'Oh, really? What makes you so special? You're just dreaming of getting money from others. Have you ever thought of creating something of your own?'

'whoa whoa whoa! What's going on here? What about returning my car key? The intruder exclaims.

In the realization that the husband and wife were oblivious to the whereabouts of the car key, Somdej pivoted his intentions towards a plan infused with malice.

'Nuch, I guess I'll have to rely on you to help restore my memory once again.'

'Fuck off'

'Wat already knows that we've been fucking before. He doesn't mind if we do it in front of him.'

'You, a perverted immoral.'

'Well, thank you for noticing! I must be doing something right if I can provoke such strong reactions. It's an art, really.' Somdej seizes her delicate wrist, swiftly propelling her onto the plush embrace of the sofa. He enfolds her in a tender embrace, planting affectionate kisses upon her—a deliberate act to incite the man tied to a chair. Twatchai turns his face away, his gaze directed elsewhere, a pained expression etched upon his features. There's a palpable ache in his heart as he avoids looking directly, as though seeking solace in the diversion, and endeavors to subtly shift both wrists, seeking liberation from the constriction that binds them.

'If you hadn't fucked up my brain, I wouldn't have to go through this pain. Do you know how agonizing it is not to remember anything? The money I've worked so hard to earn, now I don't even know where it is. If it goes missing, I'll fucking kill you all.' Somdej speaks in a harsh tone, accompanied by forceful bangs on poor Nuch. Even as Twatchai rejects her in his heart, the unfolding events before him inflict a profound ache as he witnesses his beloved wife being mistreated. He strains to unearth the appropriate words, a response to the unscrupulous deeds orchestrated by Somdej.

'Deception! the most treacherous motherfucker. Betrayer, traitor, that's who you are.'

'If you had chosen to dump me in the woods that day, things would have turned out differently.' The fleeting conversation between the married couple whispered into his semi-conscious state.

'I regret not eliminating you on that day.' Twatchai storms out in anger.

'Nobody's perfect, buddy. Look at your wife; proof you're not.' Somdej mocks and then continues, 'Business is essentially a deceitful process devoid of compassion, driven solely by self-interest. You see, my partner, Kiti, underestimates my discernment. Fortunately, I kept up with his game.' Somdej constantly bangs the wife, intending to cause emotional pain to the husband. Twatchai's anguished screams echo through the air as he contorts his body, vividly displaying the depth of his suffering to the other party. Unbeknownst to Somdej, he seizes this opportune moment to discreetly work on loosening the tightly bound ropes around his hands.

'Let go of me, you son of a bitch. Fuck you!'

Somdej burst into laughter, a sound that

echoed through the air, carrying with it a sense of contentment. In that moment, he let go of the built-up tension, allowing the lightness of joy to fill the atmosphere. His voice crescendos triumphantly as he attains the pinnacle, a deliberate effort to inflict pain upon Twatchai. This sinister crescendo is accompanied by a resurfacing tide of memories.

'The temple! The goddamn temple. That's it. The damn car is there.

In the precise moment when the rope tightens around Twatchai's wrist and loosens, Nuch seizes that opportunity, grabbing the gun Somdej has carelessly placed on the sofa. Without a second thought, she aims it at Somdej's face and pulls the trigger, the firing pin striking an empty chamber and producing a distinct clicking sound.

'Well, that's for sure. Someone like you can't be easily convinced otherwise.'

The concealed truth about the empty chamber remains unknown, a clandestine secret harbored since the beginning. In a sudden and chaotic moment, Somdej wrests the gun back from Nuch, while Twatchai fiercely topples a chair, breaking free from their entanglement. Swiftly loading bullets into the magazine, Somdej's actions prompt Twatchai to make a daring escape through the window. The sound of gunfire echoes as Somdej shoots in pursuit, but his aim falters, missing Twatchai and colliding with the window frame. Amidst the chaos, an errant bullet finds an unintended target, piercing Nuch's forehead. The report of gunfire reverberates through the quiet streets.

Simultaneously, as Kiti returns to the scene, his resolve to question the homeowner about Somdej remains firm. However, upon his arrival, the sudden echo of a gunshot reverberates from within the house, startling him. Without hesitation, he swiftly seizes the firearm, gripping it tightly in his hand. As Somdej emerges at the doorway, gun in hand, pursuing the fleeing figure, Kiti discerns his posture, sensing imminent peril. Worried about the potential of stray bullets, Kiti discharges a warning shot into the air. The moment Somdej lays eyes on Kiti, memories of the man's ruthless nature flood back. Without hesitation, Somdej takes aim and fires at Kiti. A dramatic exchange of bullets takes place between the two, eventually ending with Somdej's death, sealed by a fatal shot.

CHAPTER NINE

Following the police's meticulous inquiry into the incident, a sense of calm gradually settled over the situation. In a matter of days, Twatchai brings his novel to its conclusion, a tale woven from the fabric of real-life experiences he has weathered. The narrative seamlessly addresses every expectation of the market. Amid the process of delivering the original manuscript to the publisher, the resonant melody of his mobile phone reverberates, heralding a new chapter in the unfolding story.

The melodious voice of a young woman resonates through the mobile phone

'Is this Twatchai?'

'Yes, speaking.'

'We found the key that was supposed to be returned to you.'

'A key?'

'Yes, a car key, dropped inside your pickup truck. We held onto it during the painting process and forgot to return it to you.' Realizing that his car keys are in their rightful place with none missing. Yet, it seems to be the very key that Somdej has been desperately seeking. In a moment of recollection, he recalls the day when he chauffeured the stranger in his car. The possibility lingers that a stranger's car key might have been unintentionally dropped inside his vehicle. Instead of promptly delivering the original manuscript, he decides to make his way to the garage, intent on retrieving the misplaced key.

He reaches the garage in a flash and finds himself face to face with the woman who was on the phone.

'Hi. I'm here for the key.'

'Sure, here it is.'

Twatchai cast a contemplative gaze upon the car keys cradled in his palm, his expression reflective and deep in thought.

'I believe it belongs to you.'

'Yes, of course. It's mine.'

As the evening serenity envelops the temple, he arrives at the tranquil sanctuary, a place he has forsaken and overlooked for too long. Now, as he crosses the threshold into this hallowed sanctuary, uncertainty clouds his mind, questioning whether fate will grant him ownership of the hidden treasures. No vehicles clutter the temple grounds, a stark reminder of its sacred isolation. If he were to adhere strictly to the principles of devout Buddhism, perhaps a vehicle might indeed be awaiting him right before his eyes. His spirit sinks as he contemplates the slim chances of anyone truly striking it rich—perhaps just one fortunate soul among millions, and he, alas, does not count among them. Sitting on the chapel steps, he pulls out Somdej's car key. A petite bell adorned the keychain, catching the light and emitting a delicate tinkle when moved. As he contemplates the recent weeks, it feels as if destiny itself taunted him. Despite the desire to laugh, the pain within his heart stifles any hint of mirth. It seems fate has played a cruel joke, robbing him of everything, leaving only fragments of shattered dreams. The gentle chime of the bell reaches someone's ears, drawing an elderly, blind monk closer.

'Ah, you have returned.' Lost in the cryptic utterances of the blind monk, he trails the aged figure until they stand before a timeworn structure. A rolled-down metal door guards the secrets within. With deliberate grace, the monk unveils a forgotten relic—a car, adorned in a coat of undisturbed dust. Holding the key like a talisman, Twatchai presses the remote control, stirring the dormant vehicle to life with an obedient hum. In that moment of revelation, clarity emerges—an untouched sanctuary for Somgej's car, patiently awaiting rediscovery within the silent embrace of the hidden abode.

In this moment, he embraces the belief that fortune has favored him among the millions. With unwavering resolve, he crosses the threshold of the temple, drawn to pay reverence to the timeless and dignified Buddha statue resting upon its sacred dais. The tranquil smile adorning the Buddha's visage appears to bestow a sense of delight upon him.

Twatchai eases the car out of the temple grounds. Enveloped in an almost trance-like state, he gracefully navigates the winding roads as if under the influence of a calming elixir. The journey continues with an ethereal glide, concluding as he carefully parks the car beside the serene lake. The wavering uncertainty of destiny, with its potential for deceit, prompts him to decide to disembark from the vehicle. The ambient stillness embraces him, a solitary figure in an empty landscape. His gaze wanders to the rear, where the trunk holds its enigmatic secrets—a Pandora's box of possibilities. Is it merely an empty compartment, or does it harbor something more profound?

Curiosity drives him to uncover the mysteries hidden within the trunk. With a lift of the lid, the revelation unfolds—four travel bags, each holding a tightly packed world within. Swiftly opening one, he glimpses its contents, only to close it with the same haste. The air holds the weight of anticipation as he returns to the driver's seat.

In the sanctuary of the car, he reaches for the manuscript, feeling the textured paper beneath his fingers. On the final page, he wields a pen, crossing out the definitive "The End," and, with a stroke of determination, inscribes a new promise: "to be continued."

Charlie Nawamin

The End

About Me

As Charlie Nawamin, hailing from Thailand, I am renowned for my diverse talents as a filmmaker, producer, and writer. My cinematic journey commenced with studies at a college in Chicago, where I immersed myself in the art of filmmaking, drawing inspiration from both Eastern and Western cultures.

This novel is a testament to my creative endeavors, serving as a literary adaptation of a film bearing the same title. Initially produced in 2011, the film faced reluctance in societies that avoided open discussions about sexuality. However, upon its release in more liberal Western nations, it garnered significant acclaim and popularity.

Despite societal challenges, I persist as a prolific writer, exploring various genres from enchanting bedtime tales to gripping fiction novels. With a collection of stories already in my possession, I continue to craft narratives that captivate audiences worldwide. Stay tuned for more stories from my imagination as I start on new creative adventures in the future.

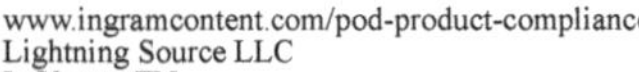

9 786166 122244